Pete the Cat

Rocking in My School Shoes

For Dr. Stephen Litwin, my father,
who told me my first stories
—E.L.

To Kim, the girl who told me she wanted to live in a small
cabin and make things out of clay
—J.D.

ISBN 978-0-545-50106-4

20 19   14 15 16 17/0

Printed in the U.S.A.   40

First Scholastic printing, September 2012

Typography by Jeanne L. Hogle

Pete the Cat

Rocking in My School Shoes

Story by Eric Litwin (aka Mr. Eric)

Art by James Dean

SCHOLASTIC INC.

Here comes Pete
strolling down the street,
rocking red shoes
on his four furry feet.

Pete is going to school,
and he sings this song:

PETE'S
LUNCH

Pete is sitting at his desk when his teacher says,
"Come on, Pete,
down that hall
to a room with books
on every wall."

The library!

Pete has never been to the library before!

Does Pete worry?
Goodness, no!

He finds his favorite book
and sings his song:

"I'm reading in my **school** shoes,

I'm reading in my **school** shoes,

I'm reading in my **school** shoes."

Check out Pete.
He's ready to eat
in a big, noisy room
with tables and seats.

Where is Pete?

It can be loud and busy in the lunchroom.

Does Pete worry?
Goodness, no!

He sits down with his friends
and sings his song:

"I'm eating in my **school** shoes,

I'm eating in my **school** shoes,

I'm eating in my **school** shoes."

Pete and his friends
    are playing outside
        on a green, grassy field
            with swings and tall slides.

Where is Pete?

Kids are running in every direction!

Does Pete worry?

Goodness, no!

He slides, and swings, and sings his song:

"I'm playing in my  **school** shoes,

I'm playing in my **school** shoes,

I'm playing in my

school shoes."

All day long Pete sings his song.

"I'm singing in my **school** shoes,

I'm painting in my **school** shoes,

I'm adding in my **school** shoes,

I'm writing in my **school** shoes."

When school is done, Pete rides
the bus home.

And I will do it again tomorrow!

Because it's all good."